I0889225

BUILT FOR SUCCESS

THE STORY OF

Lululemon Athletica

Published by Creative Education and Creative Paperbacks
P.O. Box 227, Mankato, Minnesota 56002
Creative Education and Creative Paperbacks
are imprints of The Creative Company
www.thecreativecompany.us

DESIGN BY **ZENO DESIGN**
PRODUCTION BY **TRAVIS GREEN**
ART DIRECTION BY **RITA MARSHALL**

PHOTOGRAPHS BY Alamy (Richard Levine), AP Photos (Jonathan Hayward/ASSOCIATED PRESS), Corbis (Atlantide Phototravel, Ken Cedeno, CHRIS HELGREN/Reuters, KT, BEN NELMS/Reuters, MAK REMISSA/epa, KIMBERLY WHITE/Reuters), Flickr (Krista Kennell/Fortune Most Powerful Women Summit), Getty Images (Bloomberg, Boston Globe, Stuart C. Wilson), Newscom (BROWN ADRIAN/SIPA, Suvra Kanti Das/ZUMA Press, Richard Graulich/ZUMAPRESS, RICHARD B. LEVINE, Ana Venegas/ZUMA Press), Shutterstock (Everett Collection, OlegDoroshin, Sergey Yechikov)

LIBRARY OF CONGRESS CATALOGING-IN-PUBLICATION DATA
Murray, Laura K.
The story of Lululemon Athletica / Laura K. Murray.
p. cm. — (Built for success)
Summary: A look at the origins, leaders, growth, and innovations of Lululemon Athletica, the Canadian athletic apparel company that was founded in 1998 and today has hundreds of retail locations.
Includes bibliographical references and index.
ISBN 978-1-60818-558-0 (hardcover)
ISBN 978-1-62832-159-3 (pbk)
1. Lululemon Athletica—Juvenile literature. 2. Sport clothes industry—Canada—History—Juvenile literature. I. Title.

HD9948.5.C24L856 2015
381'.4568716—dc23 2014028001

CCSS: RI.5.1, 2, 3, 8; RH.6-8.4, 5, 6, 8

BUILT FOR SUCCESS

THE STORY OF

Lululemon Athletica

LAURA K. MURRAY

It's just before 10:00 A.M., and a group of women and a few men lie on yoga mats in an otherwise empty New York Lululemon Athletica store. They are in the *savasana* pose—on their backs, with arms and legs extended. Each is wearing at least one Lululemon product. Minutes later, the instructor ends the free class, and clothing racks are pushed back into place as the store opens for the day. Soon, other customers arrive, crowding the polished aisles to examine shelves of colorful clothing and accessories. One Lululemon employee runs in place to display her $98 Groove Pant. Another trades stretching tips with a customer. The shoppers are regulars at Lululemon, a company that has made clothing into a lifestyle—and gained nearly as many critics as supporters.

CHAPTER ONE

Canada's New Clothes

When Canadian businessman Chip Wilson attended his first yoga class in the late 1990s, he knew he was on to something special. Yoga, a practice that combines mental and physical exercise, had existed in Eastern cultures for centuries. It wasn't until the 1970s, however, that it became popular in North America.

As a lifelong athlete, Wilson immediately felt a connection with yoga. But sitting in the class surrounded by mostly women, Wilson also saw a business opportunity: yoga-inspired clothing.

Wilson had many years of **retail** experience. In 1979, he had started a successful company that sold skateboarding, snowboarding, and surfing apparel. As he observed his yoga classmates dressed in baggy cotton T-shirts, he decided there should be more flattering alternatives to the limited workout clothes available to women. Wilson was on top of a trend. Over the next decade, companies such as Nike and Gap would launch their own lines of activewear made especially for women.

Wilson founded his new business, called Lululemon Athletica, in 1998. While he and his wife, Shannon, tested different clothing designs, they used the company's studio space to host evening yoga classes. Then Wilson called in the experts.

Born in 1956, Lululemon founder Chip Wilson holds a Bachelor of Arts degree in economics.

He and a small staff outfitted several Vancouver yoga teachers in Lululemon apparel. In return, the teachers offered feedback, taught free yoga classes, and promoted the **brand**. Wilson called the teachers "ambassadors." Word spread as the teachers wore the new clothes during their classes. And since Lululemon didn't rely on splashy advertising, it began to see itself as part of a **grassroots** yoga movement.

In November 2000, the first Lululemon store opened in British Columbia's trendy beach area of Kitsilano, Vancouver. "Lulu" quickly gained loyal customers who called themselves "Luluheads." Over the next few years, the company added five more stores around Canada. Wilson explained the interest in the chain by remarking, "We put together yoga-inspired athletic clothing for women that fit properly and injected some style into it." He made some of the early Lululemon stores into **franchises**.

From the beginning, Lululemon stood out from other retailers. Besides the high cost of its pants, tank tops, and other items, it was also known for offering free weekly yoga classes. But the real difference was in what Lulu represented: a way of life. Wilson wanted the target **market**—relatively wealthy women—to feel so comfortable that they would return again and again. First, Wilson tried to make the stores feel like communities. Salespeople were friendly "educators" who could answer questions about yoga and build relationships with their customers. Shoppers were called "guests."

Wilson also wanted the Lululemon brand to represent health and happiness. To develop that image, he turned to his staff. Most of the Lululemon employees were runners who enjoyed yoga. Wilson required each of them to read books and listen to recordings about how to improve their lives. Most importantly, they attended classes together to set goals. During the classes, "goal coaches" asked employees questions about what was important in their lives and what they wanted to be doing in 10 years. The staff had to display their goals on chalkboards around the store and report on their progress. They encouraged

Lululemon instructors encouraged yoga first-timers to participate in free classes and demonstrations.

customers to do the same on boards hung in the dressing rooms. Not all employees liked the unusually personal workplace—it made some uncomfortable. "They ... wanted to know so much about me," said one employee who quit.

According to Lululemon, its practices were meant "to elevate the world from mediocrity to greatness." Mediocrity meant being ordinary, and Wilson was passionate about rising above the ordinary. The company published a statement known as its manifesto, filled with advice such as "Sweat once a day" and "Dance, sing, floss, and travel." The phrases were often printed on store bags. However, some of the messages (such as one about death and another that called soft drinks "cheap drugs") caused controversy, or disagreement, and were later removed from circulation.

In 2003, Wilson decided to expand further and announced Lululemon would add a location in the United States. More people were learning yoga, and the retailer was confident it was the perfect time to bring its business strategies to the U.S. "One of the reasons that we have been so successful in Canada is that we have developed a close-knit relationship with our customers, especially local athletes and yoga instructors," said Brett Conrad, co-owner of U.S. operations. In July, Lululemon opened its 3,300-square-foot (307 sq m) store in Santa Monica, California. That same year, Lululemon won an award for being the most innovative small business in Canada.

Yogis (people who practice yoga) weren't the only ones shopping at Lululemon. Runners, bikers, dancers, and gym-goers were buying up the company's merchandise. Some bought the clothes just to wear around the house. The comfortable workout gear was often made out of Lulu's signature fabric, Luon. Besides comfort, Wilson wanted to be sure the clothes were fashionable enough to be worn all day. "He's made sweatpants and recreational apparel trendy," noted one impressed business expert. And since Lulu designers had expanded their clothing's purpose to cover more than just yoga, the company would be able to count on sales, even if interest in yoga dwindled. Such growth, however, would come with its own set of problems.

> *"The concept of a women's athletic apparel retailer has been floating around for a long time, yet thus far, [Lululemon] is the only concept to gain traction."*
>
> FAYE LANDES, ANALYST

Along with Canadian clothing company Specialized, Lululemon sponsors a women's pro cycling team.

WINNER! 2010 TONY AWARD
BEST MUSICAL
MEMPHIS
#MakeItWork
LG
TOSHIBA
TRULY AMAZED FOR THE FIRST TIME IN YEARS.
GHOST
THE MUSICAL
UNLIKE ANYTHING SEEN ONSTAGE BEFORE
TICKETMASTER.COM
MARY POPPINS
BRAVE
Disney
SOLSTICE
ATHLETA
MIND OVER MADNESS
YOGA
GUESS
ATHLETA

A POPULAR POSE

Until the 1970s, most people in North America hadn't heard of yoga. But over the next 40 years, yoga would go from a "hippie" practice to a mainstream form of exercise. Chip Wilson founded Lululemon at the perfect time to turn the new trend into a business. Other companies soon followed suit, launching their own yoga-inspired lines. Today, more than 20 million people in the U.S. practice yoga. That popularity has generated a $27-billion industry dedicated to yoga clothes, mats, shoes, towels, DVDs, and books. While many have flocked to the new practice, some are protesting the way modern yoga has departed from its spiritual roots. "It seems that inner peace comes with a high price tag," observed Bustle.com writer Claire Luchette in late 2013. But others believed clothing could encourage people to exercise and feel confident. "I see girls at ... yoga wearing Lululemon clothes, and they look the part," said psychologist and personal trainer Susan Rudnicki. "I think: 'They must be really good.'"

CHAPTER TWO

Growing Pains

Just a few years after opening its doors, Lululemon had grown at an incredible pace, adding more Canadian and American locations and opening stores in Australia and Japan as well. In 2004, it raked in **revenues** of $40.7 million.

Although the company had its share of critics who believed yoga shouldn't be turned into a business opportunity, its customers kept coming back for more, just as Wilson had hoped.

The location of each new store was chosen carefully. First, Lulu opened a "showroom" in the area, which carried just a few products. The showroom was meant to gauge if people might be interested in shopping at a Lululemon. The location was a little bit like a secret. "Showrooms are usually hidden because we want people to take the time to find us and show us they want a store here," explained Amy Klippert, a showroom **manager** in Ann Arbor, Michigan. If the location seemed promising, Lulu staff scoured fitness studios for ambassadors to create a buzz for the upcoming store. But as company-wide revenue continued to climb, Lululemon seemed to be in the spotlight just as often for controversy as for sales.

One of the earliest debates centered on how Lululemon made its clothes. The company had always prided itself on producing its clothing in Canada. But, like

Some Lululemon stores featured statues of Buddha, a key figure in both the Buddhist religion and yoga.

many North American retailers, it soon **outsourced** a portion of its manufacturing to Asia. Some criticized the decision, but Wilson explained that it was cheaper to make the clothing in overseas factories. "We have two choices," he said, "which are to manufacture everything in [Asia] … or to not be in business. You do it or die." When Lulu put an advertisement in *Yoga Journal* poking fun at **child labor**, critics did not see the humor. Wilson responded that the ad was meant to get people talking about a serious issue.

Those events fueled more bad press in 2005. At a Vancouver business conference, Wilson said that children in poor countries should be allowed to work in factories to earn money and learn skills. Many people were alarmed by this view, because child labor often involves unsafe working conditions in places known as sweatshops. In order to prove its operations were safe and **ethical**, Lululemon hired production manager Kerri McKenzie. She would be responsible for developing a code, or rules, for how Lulu made its clothes. "We're a new company that is just exploding at the seams," McKenzie told the press. By the end of the year, Lululemon had 33 locations. It also had a chief executive officer (CEO)—Wilson—who didn't have experience running such a large business.

Wilson realized he needed help. In December 2005, he sold a 48 percent stake in Lululemon to private firms Advent International and Highland Capital Partners. As part of the deal, Lulu got a new CEO named Robert Meers. Meers was the former leader of Reebok, and his experience was just what Lululemon needed. He planned to focus on adding more North American stores.

By the next year, Lululemon had moved into its new corporate headquarters building in Vancouver, and its more than 40 stores combined for sales of $149 million. Lulu's employees soon numbered nearly 1,700. On July 27, 2007, Lululemon held its initial public offering, which meant it let the public buy its shares, or parts of the company. The shares sold much higher than expected on Canada's Toronto **Stock** Exchange and the U.S.'s NASDAQ.

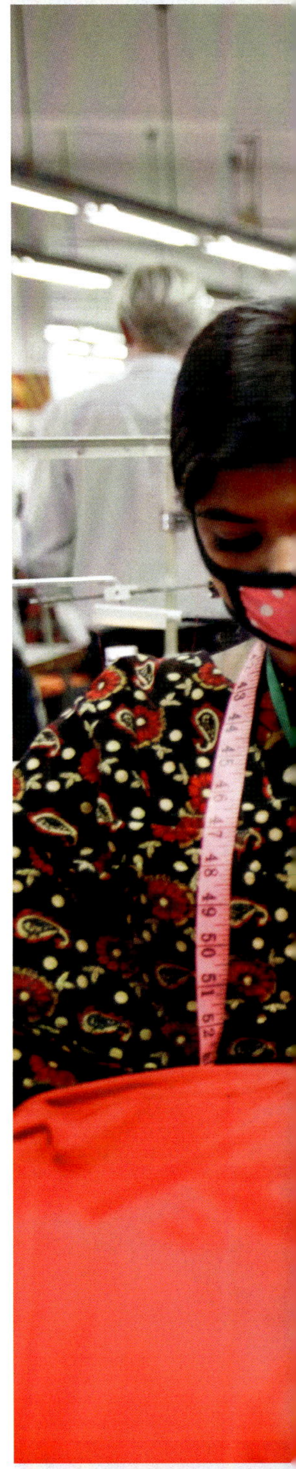

As Lulu utilized foreign factories, it made efforts to show its commitment to good working conditions.

Lululemon was clearly looking ahead to a future of growth, but some weren't sure the company was ready. Even as Lululemon's stock price soared, its stores were running out of clothes. This wasn't entirely by accident. Lulu *wanted* special products to sell out within a few weeks to make room for other items. But some customers were getting frustrated with the lack of steady merchandise. The company seemed to have grown too quickly to keep up with demand. It was a risky position for Lulu to be in, especially as new competitors had begun selling much cheaper workout apparel. While a Lululemon tank top might cost around $50 and pants upwards of $100, competitors' prices were often 50 to 75 percent less.

Loyal customers, however, felt the prices were worth it. Lululemon clothing was often made of natural materials such as bamboo and cotton. Lulu's designers had also invented several of their own special fabrics, in addition to Luon, with quirky names such as Swift, Luxtreme, and Silverescent (which reportedly contained silver to eliminate odor). Lululemon claimed that one fabric, VitaSea, was partially made with seaweed that eased stress by releasing minerals into the wearer's skin when the person sweated.

That claim prompted the *New York Times* to test VitaSea in 2007. The laboratory results came back negative for any minerals or vitamins that would indicate the usage of seaweed. Those results didn't sit well with Canada's Competition Bureau, which didn't want clothing companies making health claims. "Canadians are entitled to receive accurate information from businesses," said a bureau official. Although Wilson and Meers stood by the product, they complied with the bureau's order to remove VitaSea's stress-relieving claims. "I think every CEO of a successful public company has to learn ... that not everybody's rooting for you," Meers said afterward. Fortunately for Meers, the incident didn't seem to affect Lulu's dedicated shoppers.

"*You don't need anything to do yoga. You don't even need shoes.*"

JOHN PHILP, DOCUMENTARY FILMMAKER

Lululemon employees organized "cheering parties" for runners participating in races and marathons.

SHOP

PUTTING THE *LS* IN LULULEMON

One of the most common questions people ask Chip Wilson is where Lululemon got its name. Before starting Lulu, Wilson sold a division of one of his other companies, called Homeless Skateboards, to a Japanese buyer. He believed part of the appeal of Homeless Skateboards could be attributed to the letter *l* in its name, which made the brand seem "North American" to Japanese buyers. "I thought, 'If I ever have another company, it's going to have three *l*s in it,'" he said. After he set out to start a yoga apparel store, he and his team surveyed 100 people for their favorite names and logos from a list of choices. Voters chose the name Lululemon Athletica. The Lulu logo (a stylized *a*) came from a failed idea called Athletically Hip. But as for the triple-*l* name itself, "It means nothing," Wilson said, "other than hopefully I can get three times as much if I ever sell it."

CHAPTER THREE

Luluheads Take Over

By 2008, Lululemon had broadened its merchandise to appeal to even more customers. From hoodies and rain jackets to hats and purses, the company's 71 corporate-owned stores were offering much more than yoga apparel. In addition, more than 10 percent of Lulu's net revenue came from men's products.

The retailer again caused a stir when a Toronto news station reported a layer on some of Lulu's bags peeled off to reveal "sinister" messages about drugs and other subjects. Lululemon destroyed the remaining bags. The odd incident was just one in a string of controversies over the bags Lulu printed. Still, sales in 2008 reached $350 million despite the struggling global **economy**.

Inside Lululemon, operations were anything but smooth. Over the past three years, it had become obvious that Meers had a much different leadership style from that of Wilson. Meers also didn't fully buy into the founder's beliefs about improving lives through training sessions.

The clash had created company-wide tension. Longtime employees of Lululemon thought Meers just didn't fit in. Senior vice president of creation Deanne Schweitzer said employees weren't able to show Meers "the gift of our culture, the gift of

Lulu's popular clothing line for men included hoodies, running apparel, and golf shirts.

Lululemon." Concerned the company was losing its roots, Wilson replaced Meers with Christine Day in mid-2008 as president and CEO. Day was well known as a former executive at coffee giant Starbucks. Wilson continued as chairman of the **board of directors** and chief product designer.

Day's goal was to bring the company "back to basics." First, she addressed one of the main concerns of **shareholders** and made sure Lulu had the structure to support its growth. Then, to gather customer feedback, Day went right to the source. She spent hours inside Lulu stores, listening for complaints. Employees also were positioned near fitting rooms to overhear customers.

In response to the most commonly perceived flaws, Day tweaked the products and sometimes even lowered prices. Unlike many **executives**, she welcomed negative comments. "If they aren't out there complaining, I'd actually worry more because it says they've found something else," she said. She shared Wilson's cooperative vision and let local store managers make their own decisions on things such as displays. The stores were designed to look like slightly messy boutiques (high-end, small stores), each with its own feel.

Day also capitalized on Lululemon's limited supply of merchandise. The "scarcity model" became a secret weapon that brought even more customers into the stores because the products were available only for a short time. It also meant the company almost never put items on sale. In fact, rather than use the word "sale," Lulu instead labeled marked-down items as "We made too much." While many stores offered deep discounts, Lulu sold about 95 percent of its apparel at full price. It only made the Luluheads spend more money. "Our guest knows that there's a limited supply, and it creates these fanatical shoppers," Day later said.

Those fanatical shoppers were earning the company lots of attention. Business researchers were fascinated by Lululemon's unusual practices and its adoring customers who were willing to pay so much for workout pants.

Christine Day believed that building community among customers and employees would lead to success.

"It's the first time I've heard of anyone almost directly using the techniques of **cults** and applying them to their business," said author Douglas Atkin. In *New York* magazine, Bryant Urstadt added, "Even if it isn't really, truly a cult, there are aspects of the corporation that certainly ring with a cultlike air." A former employee even called the work environment "a happy cult." At any rate, the results were impressive. Lululemon was bringing in about three times more in sales per square foot (0.09 sq m) of retail space than competitors such as Abercrombie & Fitch. And Lululemon was accomplishing this feat with very little advertising. Instead, it relied on devoted customers and ambassadors to boost sales.

By now, the company had more than 900 ambassadors promoting its brand. Ambassadors got their pictures posted on Lulu's website and hung in local stores, which helped them build their own businesses. Lululemon also convinced doubters, such as one Olympic trainer, to become ambassadors by providing them with free workout gear. Wilson's entire staff was trained in the message of a best-selling book called *The Secret* by Rhonda Byrne. According to the book, positive thinking would lead to happiness, wealth, and health.

Positive thinking certainly seemed to be working for Lululemon. In the first **quarter** of 2009, Lulu reported $81.7 million in revenues. As customers of all ages visited the store, executives realized there might be a whole new market for workout apparel: young girls. In November, the company launched a high-end retail store for younger clientele. Located in Vancouver, Ivivva (*ih-VEE-vah*) Athletica was known as Lululemon's "sister." The company used its signature special fabrics, such as Luon, but made the clothing in sizes for girls ages 4 to 14. Selling leggings, headbands, sports bras, pants, and tops, the Ivivva brand focused on the ideas of community and health, just like Lululemon. It quickly labeled its customers "Ivivva girls" and described them as "active girls who love to sweat and who are all about creating their best lives possible."

"Lululemon is very image conscious. That's why women are shelling out $100 for a pair of pants they could get at Target for $20."

MARGARET BOGENRIEF,
BOUTIQUE FINANCIAL ADVISER

Best-selling (but much-criticized) author Rhonda Byrne told readers to "ask, believe, receive."

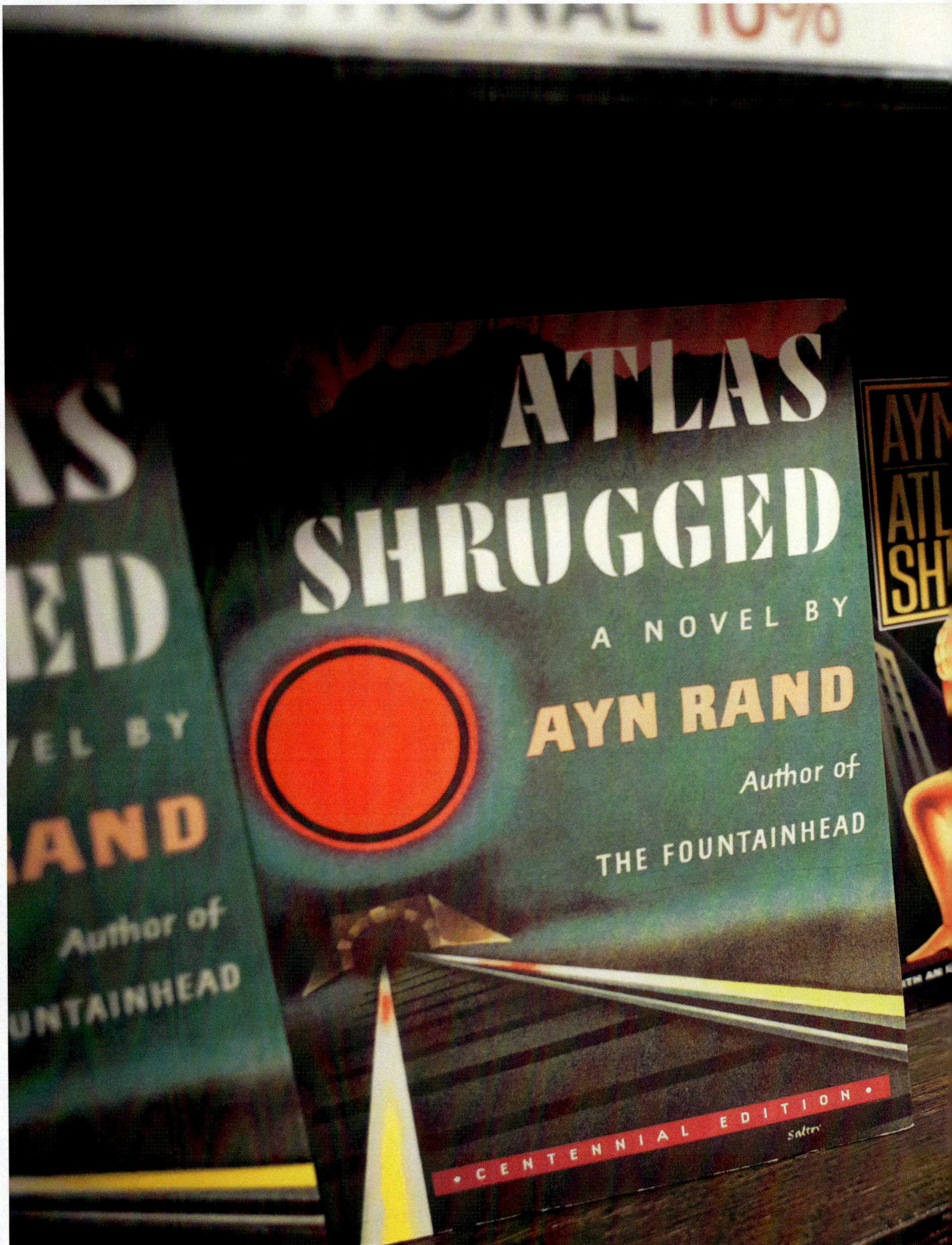
ATLAS
SHRUGGED
A NOVEL BY
AYN RAND
Author of
THE FOUNTAINHEAD
CENTENNIAL EDITION

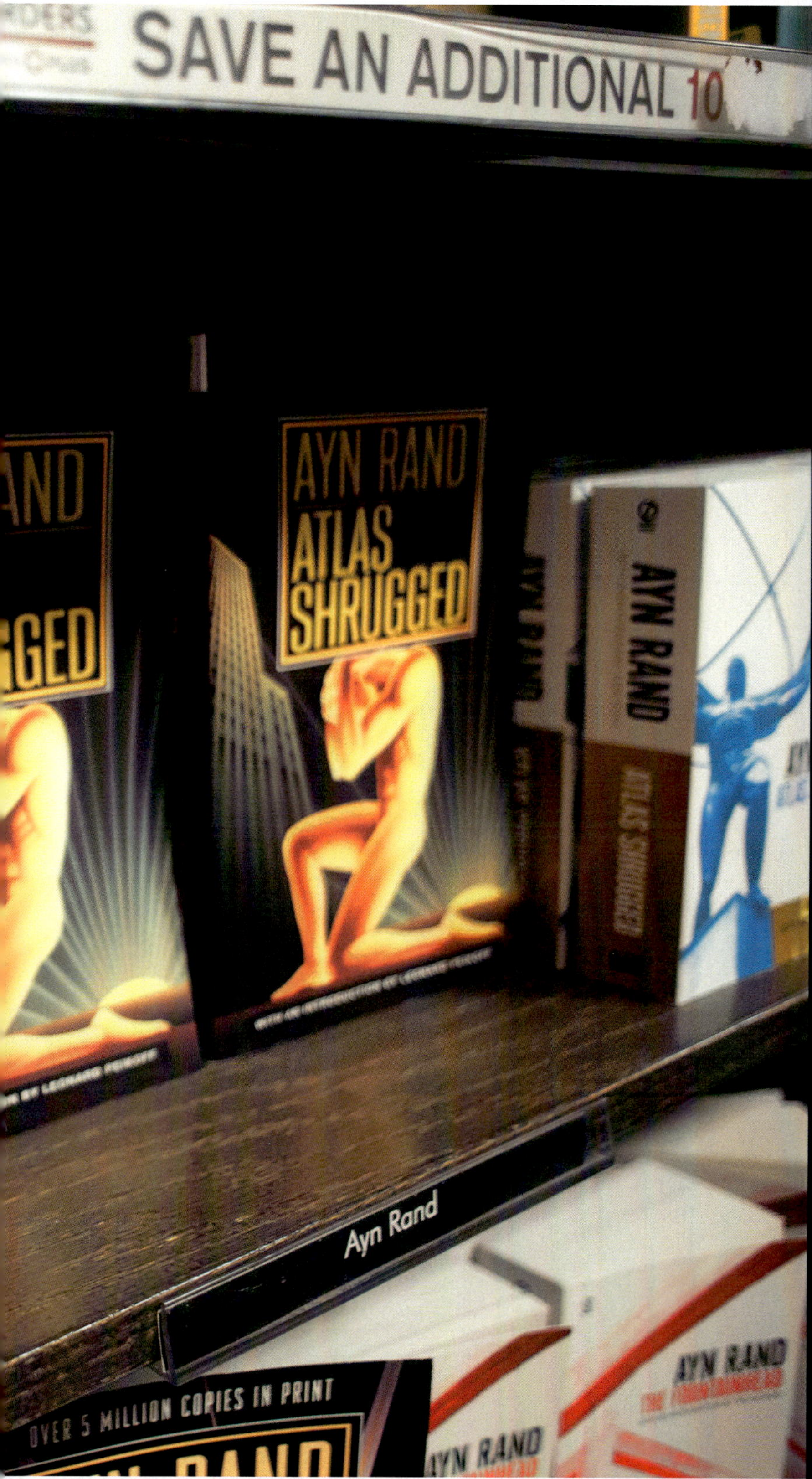

PROBLEMS WITH JOHN GALT

When Lululemon printed "Who is John Galt?" on its shopping bags in 2011, the company once again stirred up controversy. The famous phrase (and character) comes from the 1957 novel *Atlas Shrugged* by Ayn Rand, a favorite of Lululemon founder Chip Wilson's. The book promotes an individualistic way of life and suggests that the world would be a better place if everyone were left to his or her own devices. The question, though, was also used as a catchphrase in a contemporary American political movement known as the Tea Party, causing some to wonder whether Lulu was making a political statement. In response, Lululemon blogged that *Atlas Shrugged* simply went hand-in-hand with Lulu's mission of rising above the ordinary. Still, *Forbes* accused Lulu of showing "a genuine disrespect towards customers" by even printing the bags, and others argued that the divisive phrase had no place in the unity-focused practice of yoga.

CHAPTER FOUR

Stretching to the Top

As Lululemon expanded its operations close to home, it was also hard at work across the ocean. In 2010, Lululemon had 137 stores in North America and Australia (having left the Japanese market a few years before). Lulu had also become majority owner of the Australian company New Harbour Yoga.

In December, Lululemon **recalled** a number of its signature red-and-white bags from Lulu and Ivivva stores. The company was concerned the reusable bags it had been giving out for the past year contained unsafe amounts of lead. Critics accused the company of waiting too long to inform the public of the problem. Just a few months later, Lulu would have a much worse **public relations** nightmare on its hands when one of its own employees murdered another inside a Lulu store.

Of course, nothing could deter Luluheads from shopping, and Lululemon was named one of *Fortune*'s fastest-growing companies of 2011. To control all the locations of its popular brand, Lululemon bought back its last franchise stores. It also improved its online shopping options. After launching online Ivivva products, Lululemon overhauled its own website. Soon, the company was generating 10 percent of its revenue through online sales. Blogs and personal websites about Lulu

Designed for easy movement, Ivivva products for girls featured vibrant colors and eye-catching patterns.

also popped up, which allowed Luluheads to discuss clothing and workouts. Although Lululemon remained focused on the female customer, its men's line had achieved its highest sales totals yet.

The company had another leadership change in January 2012 when Wilson decided to step down from his executive position. "I was actually doing a very mediocre job of being an employee and a mediocre job of being a chairman of the board," he admitted. While he remained on the board, he left the day-to-day operations to others. Soon after, Lululemon announced it had hit $1 billion in annual sales for the first time ever.

Despite Lulu's successful sales, the stores' inability to keep items on the shelves persisted. According to chief product officer Sheree Waterson, a new color called "Paris Pink" was expected to last for two months—but it sold out in one week. As a result, the company missed out on important sales opportunities. Often, Lulu's sold-out merchandise later appeared on eBay, selling for three times more than its original price tag. Lululemon hadn't yet struck the right balance between stocking just enough items to keep customers excited and yet sufficient to make money. When the company finally increased its **inventory**, nervous shareholders breathed sighs of relief. "Imagine what the retailer can do now that it actually has enough product," wrote Abram Brown in *Forbes*.

Besides posting record sales, Lululemon was also outpacing competitors. Gap, Under Armour, and Victoria's Secret had all launched similar athletic clothing lines for women—and they knew Lulu was the one to beat. Old Navy even posted a sign reading, "Our guru thinks you're lulu if you spend $90 on yoga pants." In addition to lower prices, competitors often had friendlier store policies. For example, Lululemon accepted returns (unwashed, unworn, and with tags) only within 14 days of purchase. But other stores didn't have Lulu's carefully strategized image of health and luxury, either. "Competitors were slow to catch on to the fact that Lulu wasn't selling workout clothes so much as they were selling membership to a club with a very appealing uniform," observed

Old Navy (owned by Gap Inc.) saw sales increase once it began offering more athletic wear.

Canadian Business. "But so far, Lululemon's irresistible promises are exactly what its consumers want to hear—what they're desperate to believe."

Lululemon was paying close attention to competitors, and it was ready for battle. In September, Lulu sued Calvin Klein, another high-end clothing company. Lulu claimed Calvin Klein had copied its **patented** Astro Pant ($98) design that featured an overlapping waistband. Calvin Klein was selling a similar pant for nearly $40 cheaper. The case was unusual because, historically, fashion companies had rarely been granted patents for designs. In Lulu's case, industry experts were divided on whether legal action was appropriate. According to Ilse Metchek, president of the California Fashion Association, "This whole notion that you'd grant a patent to anyone who adds a seam or two to a waistband is quite problematic." A few months later, the two companies settled the lawsuit, but the terms of the deal were kept secret.

By early 2013, Lululemon had 211 stores in North America, Australia, and New Zealand, including 8 Canadian Ivivva stores. Ivivva showrooms were also popping up around the U.S. Shares in Lululemon stock, which sold under "LULU" (in the U.S.) and "LLL" (in Canada), had grown by more than 400 percent since 2008. The growth was largely credited to Day's leadership. But as the brand grew, so did the ranks of critics. They accused the company of being phony, ruining yoga, and promoting a body image that excluded many people.

A number of potential customers did not feel welcome in "Lululand," as the press nicknamed Lululemon's community. The retailer advertised its women's sizes as being 2 through 12. According to former employees, however, anything over a size 8 oftentimes was nowhere to be found in a store. Critics believed this was more than a simple inventory or supply problem. They thought that Lulu's messages of body acceptance and health were ringing insincere.

Despite Lululemon's cult following and growing band of critics, the brand was not yet a household name. Since Lulu didn't use traditional advertising, many people had no idea the retailer even existed. That was about to change.

> *"You really can't go wrong with this top.... I own about 15 of these and wear both to the gym and casually."*
>
> CAROLYN BEAUCHESNE,
> *LULULEMON ADDICT* BLOGGER

Calvin Klein Inc. includes many brands, from jeans and underwear to sportswear and perfume.

MURDER AT LULULEMON

Lululemon prides itself on lifting the world to greatness. But in one store, tragedy reigned instead. In 2011, employee Brittany Norwood murdered coworker Jayna Murray in a Bethesda, Maryland, Lululemon store. Employees at a nearby Apple store heard cries for help but didn't call the police. Norwood first claimed she had also been attacked by two men and even tied herself up as "proof." As the community panicked, investigators quickly realized things were not as they seemed. Norwood soon admitted to the savage killing. "A dark cloud has been cast over my heart," a friend of Murray's said at the trial. Norwood was convicted of first-degree murder and sentenced to life in prison. The brutality and unusual location made the murder infamous. Several books have been written analyzing the event, including one by *Washington Post* crime reporter Dan Morse.

CHAPTER FIVE

Lulu's Disastrous Year

Since opening its first store, Lululemon had emerged from several controversies intact. But its mistakes of 2013 would threaten its entire yoga empire. Though Lulu had had quality problems in the past (some of its colored clothing bled, while certain swimwear became see-through when wet), things took a turn for the worse in March 2013.

That month, customer complaints about its signature black Luon yoga pants skyrocketed. As it turned out, the pants became sheer once the wearer began moving in them—and that person usually had to be informed by someone else that the pants were see-through. Lulu recalled the product in a move that would cost the company $60 million. "The fact that the pants actually had to reach the customer with the problem, that's really unheard of," said Mark Sunderland, a textile engineering professor. The Luon fabric had been manufactured in Vietnam and Taiwan.

A few months later, the retailer came under fire again. Events in Cambodia turned violent as workers protested wages and working conditions at a factory that produced garments for Nike and Lululemon. The issue of overseas labor

Cambodian garment workers took to the streets in 2013 and 2014 to demand labor improvements.

conditions had been brought to the forefront by the collapse of a Bangladesh factory (not belonging to Lululemon) in April that killed more than 1,100.

The controversies had taken a toll on Lulu's leadership. Wilson and Day no longer saw eye-to-eye. Meanwhile, Luluheads called on Day to resign, blaming her for the decline of Lululemon's quality. Shareholders didn't agree with that assessment. When Day announced her resignation in June, Lulu stock plummeted.

One problem seemed to lead to another. Soon, shareholders sued Lululemon for allegedly hiding problems with the yoga pants and concealing plans to replace Day. Lulu was already facing another lawsuit that accused the retailer of increasing its executives' bonuses just before the costly pants product recall.

Several past Lulu supporters were also targeting the retailer in the press. In the *Huffington Post*, former employee Elizabeth Licorish claimed Lulu had created a bizarre work environment and looked down on certain body types. She reported that larger clothing sizes were "thrown in a heap" at the back of the store. If people hadn't heard of Lululemon before, many of them certainly had by now.

One Dallas, Texas, Lululemon store didn't help matters. In October, the store posted a breezy message in its window letting customers know it wasn't participating in a promotional discount program benefitting The Family Place, an organization that helps survivors of domestic violence. Many took offense, and Lulu eventually donated $10,000 to the charity.

In November, Lululemon made what might have been its biggest misstep yet. When customers complained their Luon yoga pants were wearing out quickly and pilling, Wilson responded by suggesting the problem was not with the pants but with the wearer. "Quite frankly, some women's bodies just actually don't work for it," he told Bloomberg TV. The remarks caused instant uproar. As one user posted to Lulu's Facebook page, the same company that preached love and positive body image was now telling customers what they could—and couldn't—wear.

Breathing is one of the principles of yoga, along with relaxation, diet, exercise, and positive thinking.

Wilson announced in December that he would step down as chairman. (He remained on the board through January 2015.) Board member Michael Casey replaced Wilson as chairman, while Laurent Potdevin, former president of Toms shoes, took over the next month as CEO. Executives were well aware that Lulu needed to do some serious rebuilding. "What doesn't kill you makes you stronger," quoted chief financial officer John Currie. "I'm joking, but not really." Still, many Luluheads seemed as devoted as ever. As journalist Stewart J. Lawrence pointed out, Lulu "seems to have nine lives when it comes to recurring **scandal** and controversy."

To regroup from the nightmarish year, the retailer focused on younger customers by expanding its streetwear and the Ivivva brand. With more than 250 stores in Canada, the U.S., Australia, and New Zealand, Lululemon also planned to open 20 stores in Europe and Asia by 2017 and its first men's-only store in 2016. As Lulu's sales strengthened slightly, the fashion industry was undergoing a major shift: denim sales were giving way to yoga pants as women's everyday wear. This was good news for the retailer, but competitors were often outdoing the regrouping Lulu when it came to recognizing new trends and getting clothing to store shelves.

After a spat with the board in June 2014, Wilson agreed to sell half of his 27-percent stake in the company to Advent International. (Advent had ended its previous involvement with Lulu in 2009.) The $834-million deal made Advent's David Mussafer cochair of the board. Between March 2013 and September 2014, Lululemon shares had dropped more than 40 percent. But in mid-September, the new leadership delivered good news: quarterly revenue—and stock prices—were up and poised to climb.

When Lulu was founded in 1998, it promised a revolution. Ever since, Lululemon has been selling more than clothing—it has been selling a way of life. That smart strategy, along with a base of loyal customers and employees, has helped the company survive a number of trials. As Lulu expands its target market, it remains to be seen whether Lululemon's best days are behind it, or if its trendsetting ways will help prove its worth as a top company.

"The truth of the matter is, the only way you can actually test for the [sheerness] is to put the pants on and bend over."

CHRISTINE DAY, FORMER LULULEMON CEO

Credited for his role in taking Lulu public, John Currie announced his retirement in 2014.

OUTFITS FOR OCEAN

As designers create Lululemon's "technology-enhanced" clothing, they find it helpful to have a muse, or inspiration. So they invented a fictional woman named Ocean. As the ideal Lululemon customer, Ocean is an educated, 32-year-old woman who makes lots of money. Lulu's senior vice president of global brand and community Laura Klauberg described Ocean as someone who is "super athletic ... who practices yoga, who probably is a runner, very successful in her career." When Lulu added men's products, they created a male muse, Ocean's 34-year-old husband Duke. (Before that, Ocean dated a triathlete named Mountain.) Lululemon designers also do morning yoga together to get the creative juices flowing. "Some designers pull inspiration from fashion," said one accessories designer, "but I'm inspired by the spaces and places that I see when I'm out getting sweaty.... I've had some of my best thoughts in savasana." Also known as the corpse pose, savasana is meant to bring total relaxation.

GLOSSARY

board of directors a group of people in charge of making decisions for a publicly owned company

brand the name of a product or manufacturer; a brand distinguishes a product from similar products made by other manufacturers

child labor the illegal use of children in business

cults groups that manipulate the beliefs or control the practices of their members

economy the system of producing, distributing, and consuming of goods within a society

ethical relating to moral principles

executives decision-making leaders of a company, such as the president or chief executive officer (CEO)

franchises businesses allowed to carry out certain activities under another company's name

grassroots starting at a basic level

inventory the total goods in stock

manager a person responsible for controlling all or parts of a company's operations

market a geographic region or segment of the population to which companies try to appeal

outsourced used an outside or foreign supplier to receive goods or perform services

patented having government-granted rights that allow an individual or company to make, use, or sell specific products or technology

public relations the practice of establishing and maintaining a favorable connection between a company and the public

quarter one of four three-month intervals that together comprise the financial year

recalled called back, or asked customers to return, all copies of a product that might be defective

retail the sale of goods

revenues the money earned by a company; another word for income

scandal an action or event that is morally or legally wrong and upsets people

shareholders people or corporations who own shares of stock (portions of ownership in a corporation)

stock shared ownership in a company by many people who buy shares, or portions, of stock, hoping the company will make a profit and the stock value will increase

SELECTED BIBLIOGRAPHY

Deveau, Scott. "Yoga Mogul Has Critics in a Knot." *The Tyee*, February 17, 2005. http://thetyee.ca/News/2005/02/17/LuluCritics/.

Gregoire, Carolyn. "How Yoga Became a $27-Billion Industry—and Reinvented American Spirituality." *Huffington Post*, December 16, 2013. http://www.huffingtonpost.com/2013/12/16/how-the-yoga-industry-los_n_4441767.html.

Kowitt, Beth, and Colleen Leahey. "Do You Speak Lululemon?" *Fortune*, August 29, 2013. http://fortune.com/2013/08/29/do-you-speak-lululemon/.

Lululemon Athletica. "Lululemon Athletica: Our Company History." http://www.lululemon.com/about/history.

Nelson, Jacqueline. "Loco for Lulu." *Canadian Business*, April 29, 2011. http://www.canadianbusiness.com/lifestyle/loco-for-lulu/.

Sacks, Danielle. "Lululemon's Cult of Selling." *Fast Company*, April 1, 2009. http://www.fastcompany.com/1208950/lululemon's-cult-selling.

Strauss, Marina. "Lululemon's Christine Day: In Sweaty Pursuit of Innovation." *The Globe and Mail*, March 8, 2013. http://www.theglobeandmail.com/report-on-business/careers/careers-leadership/lululemons-christine-day-in-sweaty-pursuit-of-innovation/article9559457/.

Urstadt, Bryant. "Lust for Lulu: How the Yoga Brand Lululemon Turned Fitness into a Spectator Sport." *New York*, July 26, 2009. http://nymag.com/shopping/features/58082/.

Note: Every effort has been made to ensure that any websites listed above were active at the time of publication. However, because of the nature of the Internet, it is impossible to guarantee that these sites will remain active indefinitely or that their contents will not be altered.

INDEX